My
Daddy's
Mustache

My Daddy's Mustache

By Naomi Panush Salus
Pictures by Tomie de Paola

Doubleday & Company, Inc. Garden City, New York

Library of Congress Catalog Number 78-68363
ISBN 0-385-13188-7 Trade
ISBN 0-385-13189-5 Prebound

For Danielle, R. J., and Stan; and for my mother and my daddy with the elephants.

Once upon a time,
long before it was fashionable
(or I was born)
my daddy grew a mustache.

He was still very attached to it
when he married my mother.
She has never seen him without it.

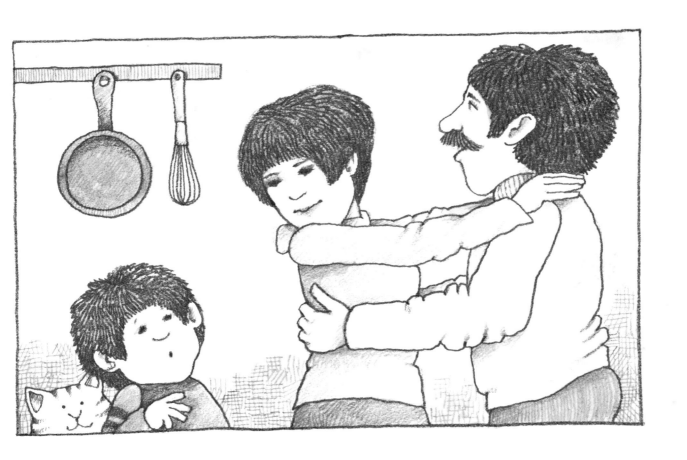

"How *can* you stand it?"
I ask her all the time.
"Don't you ever wonder
what he'd look like without it?"

"I am tickled by it," she says.

"Won't you shave it off just once?"
I beg my daddy
while I watch him shaving
in the morning.

But he just trims his mustache carefully
into a smile.

Then he answers me
just as he answered my older sisters.
He tells me why, through all the years,
through thick and thin,
he keeps it.

"It's for the elephants," he says.
"I am keeping them warm!"

Then I crawl up into his lap,
and cuddle,
and I have only to lift a hair of his mustache
to know he speaks the truth.

I see them!

Elephants—mothers, fathers, and babies—
parade by,
with trunks locked to tails,
just like in the circus.

"Why elephants?" I giggle.
"Why not walruses?"

"I do not have a walrus mustache.
A walrus mustache looks like this . . ."

"But what if a tiger were to
settle in there?"

"There's a sign that says,
'No Tigers Allowed.'"

"Why elephants?" I ask.
"Why not parrots?"

"They never asked me for a home."

"Did you ever invite penguins?"

"It's too warm for them in *this* jungle."

"But why elephants?
Why not cows?"

"It's not a moo-stache."

"What about cats?"

"It's not a mew-stache."

"Mice?"

"It's not a mouse-tache.
Mice have whiskers of their own."

His answers seem reasonable to me.
And who am I to complain?
I wish everyone I know
could have a father with elephants.

And though my daddy will never admit it,
I think the reason he keeps
the elephants is because
no one else does.

And besides,

my daddy likes to have me
cuddled in his lap.

NAOMI PANUSH SALUS was born in Detroit, Michigan, and grew up as the youngest of four girls. She graduated with honors from the University of Michigan and studied law at the American University Washington College of Law. She now works in the press office of the Board of Governors of the Federal Reserve System, where she writes and edits educational materials about monetary policy and consumer credit. She and her husband, an attorney, and their two children, Danielle and R. J., live in Washington, D.C.—and her father still keeps elephants in his mustache for his grandchildren.

TOMIE DE PAOLA grew up in Meriden, Connecticut. He studied art at Pratt Institute in Brooklyn, and later received an M.F.A. from the California College of Arts and Crafts in Oakland and a doctoral equivalency degree from Lone Mountain College in San Francisco. He has taught in California, Massachusetts, and New Hampshire, where he is now professor of visual arts at New England College in Henniker. Mr. de Paola has written and illustrated dozens of children's books, one of which, *Strega Nona,* was a Caldecott Honor Book.